P9-ASC-333

# GOODNIGHT,
## BUTTERFLY

munch

'munch

'munch

Shorewood-Troy Public Library
650 Deerwood Drive
Shorewood, IL 60404
815-725-1715
www.shorewoodtroylibrary.org

## Ross Burach

Scholastic Press  New York

I CAN'T SLEEP!!! I have SO MANY questions!!

Have you ever seen a shooting star?

What did you wish for?

I'd wish for it to rain JELLYBEANS!!!

Ever seen a cow jumping over the moon?

Can cows even jump?

Are you friends with fireflies?

When I can't sleep, nothing comforts me more than a good book!
GOOD MORNING SUN
GOOD MORNING SUN
Great idea!

SQUISH!
GOOD MORNING SUN
GOOD MORNING SUN
NEVER MIND! This book is not comforting.

Who needs to sleep at night, anyway?! There's so much I'd miss. I'll just be nocturnal, too!
This will be great!
We'll become BEST BUDS!
I've got BIG PLANS for us!
Can I borrow a quill? Thanks.
scribble
scribble
scribble
INK

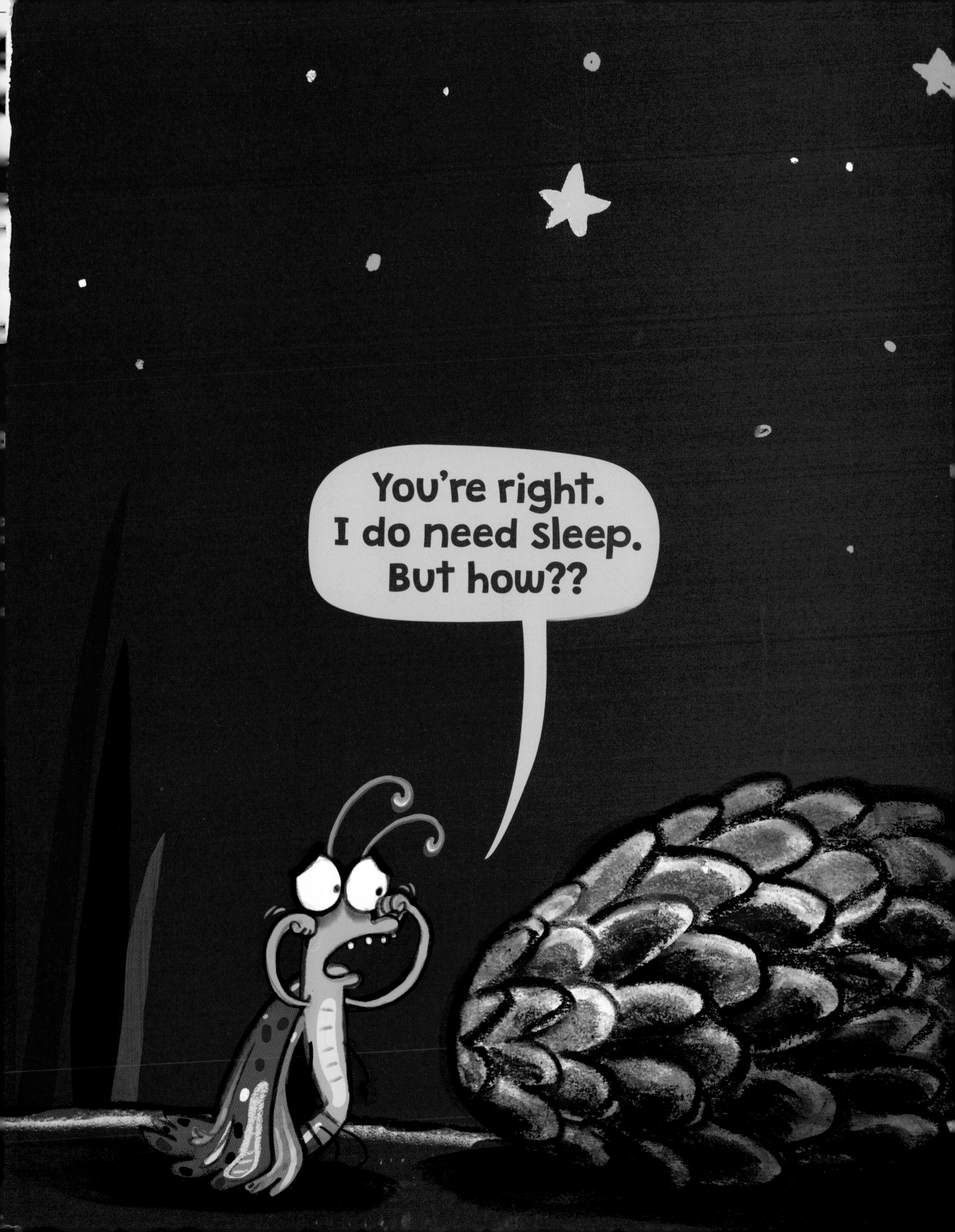
You're right.
I do need sleep.
But how??

Right. Right. Calming thoughts. Think calming thoughts.

Like . . . the calming scent of flowers?

Yes.

The sun on my wings?

Yes. What else?

The peaceful palette of springtime.

The soothing sounds of hummingbirds.

YAAWWWWWWN!!

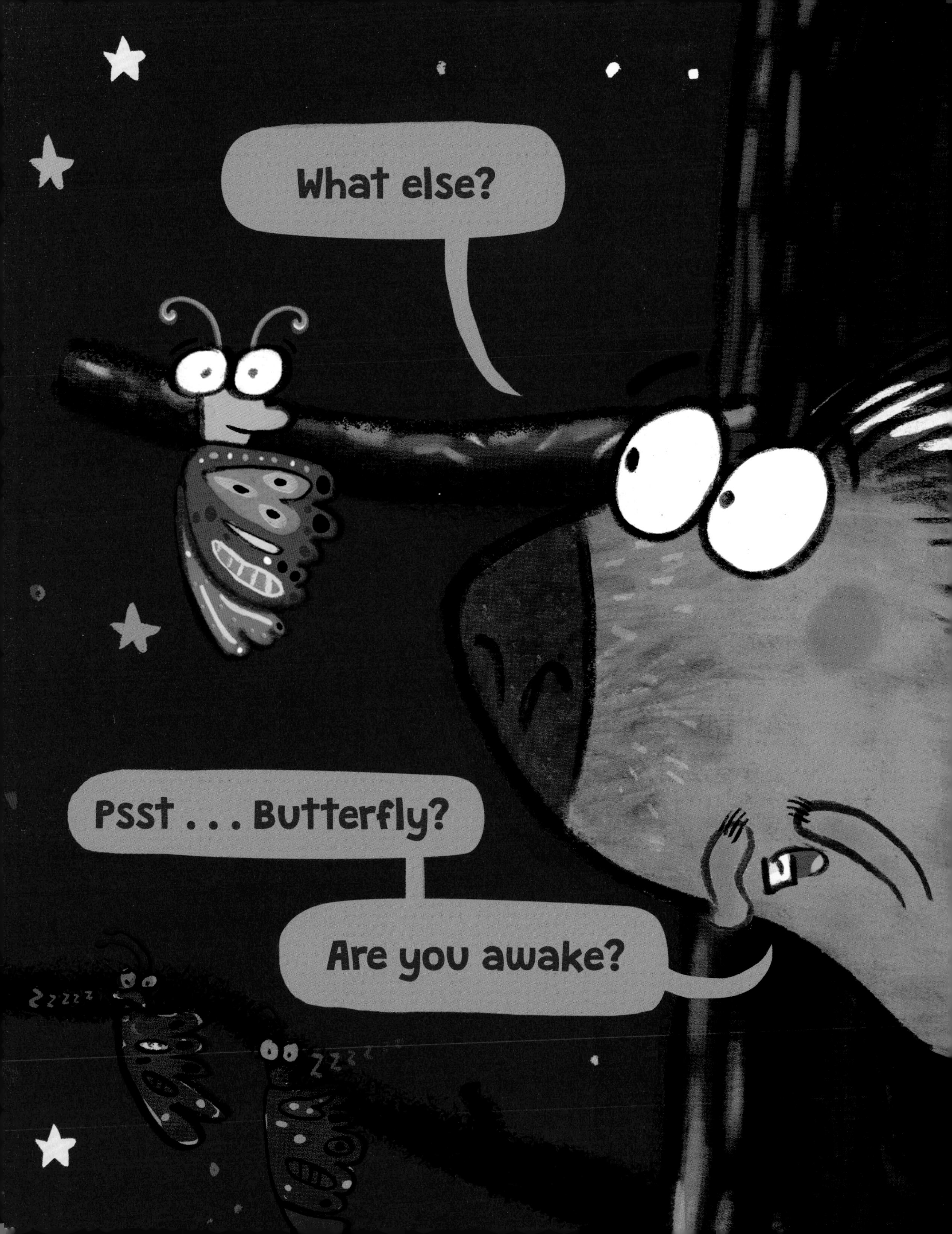
What else?
Psst . . . Butterfly?
Are you awake?
zzzzz
zzzz

To Tracy, Marijka, and Ben for keeping Butterfly flying!

Copyright © 2022 by Ross Burach · All rights reserved. Published by Scholastic Press, an imprint of Scholastic Inc., *Publishers since 1920.* SCHOLASTIC, SCHOLASTIC PRESS, and associated logos are trademarks and/or registered trademarks of Scholastic Inc. · The publisher does not have any control over and does not assume any responsibility for author or third-party websites or their content. · No part of this publication may be reproduced, stored in a retrieval system, or transmitted in any form or by any means, electronic, mechanical, photocopying, recording, or otherwise, without written permission of the publisher. For information regarding permission, write to Scholastic Inc., Attention: Permissions Department, 557 Broadway, New York, NY 10012. · This book is a work of fiction. Names, characters, places, and incidents are either the product of the author's imagination or are used fictitiously, and any resemblance to actual persons, living or dead, business establishments, events, or locales is entirely coincidental. · Library of Congress Cataloging-in-Publication Data available · ISBN 978-1-338-61501-2 · 10 9 8 7 6 5 4 3      22 23 24 25 26 · Printed in India      202 · First edition, August 2022

Ross Burach's art was created with pencil, crayon, acrylic paint, and digital coloring. · The text type was set in Grandstander Classic Bold. · The display type was set in Grandstander Classic Bold. The book was printed on 157gsm Kinmari matt paper and bound at RR Donnelly Asia. · Production was overseen by Catherine Weening. · Manufacturing was supervised by Shannon Rice. The book was art directed and designed by Marijka Kostiw, and edited by Tracy Mack.